Dear Parents:

Congratulations! Your child is taking the first steps on an exciting journey. The destination? Independent reading!

STEP INTO READING® will help your child get there. The program offers five steps to reading success. Each step includes fun stories and colorful art or photographs. In addition to original fiction and books with favorite characters, there are Step into Reading Non-Fiction Readers, Phonics Readers and Boxed Sets, Sticker Readers, and Comic Readers—a complete literacy program with something to interest every child.

Learning to Read, Step by Step!

Ready to Read   Preschool–Kindergarten
• big type and easy words • rhyme and rhythm • picture clues
For children who know the alphabet and are eager to begin reading.

Reading with Help   Preschool–Grade 1
• basic vocabulary • short sentences • simple stories
For children who recognize familiar words and sound out new words with help.

Reading on Your Own   Grades 1–3
• engaging characters • easy-to-follow plots • popular topics
For children who are ready to read on their own.

Reading Paragraphs   Grades 2–3
• challenging vocabulary • short paragraphs • exciting stories
For newly independent readers who read simple sentences with confidence.

Ready for Chapters   Grades 2–4
• chapters • longer paragraphs • full-color art
For children who want to take the plunge into chapter books but still like colorful pictures.

STEP INTO READING® is designed to give every child a successful reading experience. The grade levels are only guides; children will progress through the steps at their own speed, developing confidence in their reading.

Remember, a lifetime love of reading starts with a single step!

© 2020 Viacom International Inc. All rights reserved. Published in the United States by Random House Children's Books, a division of Penguin Random House LLC, 1745 Broadway, New York, NY 10019, and in Canada by Penguin Random House Canada Limited, Toronto. Series © 2018–19 Nelvana Limited. Nelvana is a trademark of the Corus Entertainment group of companies. All rights reserved. Nickelodeon, Nick Jr., Corn & Peg, and all related titles, logos, and characters are trademarks of Viacom International Inc.

Step into Reading, Random House, and the Random House colophon are registered trademarks of Penguin Random House LLC.

Visit us on the Web!
StepIntoReading.com
rhcbooks.com

Educators and librarians, for a variety of teaching tools, visit us at RHTeachersLibrarians.com

ISBN 978-0-593-12395-9 (trade) — ISBN 978-0-593-12396-6 (lib. bdg.)

Printed in the United States of America   10 9 8 7 6 5 4 3 2 1

Random House Children's Books supports the First Amendment and celebrates the right to read.

THE GREEN TEAM!

adapted by Lauren Clauss

based on the teleplay "The Great Earth Day Gallop" by Patrick Granleese

illustrated by Erik Doescher

Random House 🏠 New York

Corn and Peg
are best friends.
They like
to do good.

It is Earth Day!
The town is having
a race in nature.

The winner gets
the Earth Day Cup!

The race starts.

Corn and Peg
are very fast!
They are in front.

There are flowers
in the path.
Corn and Peg
stop to do good.

They build a fence
to protect the flowers.

The other runners
pass them.

Corn and Peg

join the race again.

They catch up!

They see trash.
They stop to
do good and
clean it up.

The other runners
pass them again.

Corn and Peg
join the race again.
They catch up!

They reach the river.

The water is orange.

Corn and Peg
stop to do good.
They clean up the river.
The other runners
pass them again.

Corn and Peg
run to the finish line.
Everyone else has
stopped racing.

They know Corn and Peg
helped nature.

Corn and Peg
win the race!

They plant
the little tree
from their cup
in the park.

Doing good
feels good!